For the Rovers: Brian, Lissa, and Marcus
—D.S.

For my mom
—S.H.

Farrar Straus Giroux Books for Young Readers
An imprint of Macmillan Publishing Group, LLC
175 Fifth Avenue, New York, NY 10010

Text copyright © 2017 by Dashka Slater
Pictures copyright © 2017 by Sydney Hanson
All rights reserved
Color separations by Embassy Graphics
Printed in China by RR Donnelley Asia Printing Solutions Ltd., Dongguan City, Guangdong Province.
First edition, 2017
5 7 9 10 8 6

mackids.com

Library of Congress Cataloging-in-Publication Data

Names: Slater, Dashka, author. | Hanson, Sydney, illustrator.
Title: Escargot / Dashka Slater ; pictures by Sydney Hanson.
Description: First edition. | New York : Farrar Straus Giroux, 2017. | Summary: Escargot is a beautiful French snail who only wants
   to be your favorite animal and get to the delicious salad at the end of the book, even if he has to try a carrot, which he hates.
Identifiers: LCCN 2016024331 | ISBN 9780374302818 (hardcover)
Subjects: | CYAC: Snails—Fiction. | Humorous stories. | BISAC: JUVENILE FICTION / Animals / Insects, Spiders, etc. |
   JUVENILE FICTION / Social Issues / New Experience. | JUVENILE FICTION / Humorous Stories.
Classification: LCC PZ7.S62897 Es 2017 | DDC [E]—dc23
LC record available at https://lccn.loc.gov/2016024331

Our books may be purchased in bulk for promotional, educational, or business use. Please contact your local bookseller or the Macmillan
Corporate and Premium Sales Department at (800) 221-7945 ext. 5442 or by e-mail at MacmillanSpecialMarkets@macmillan.com.

Escargot

STORY BY Dashka Slater

PICTURES BY Sydney Hanson

FARRAR STRAUS GIROUX · NEW YORK

Bonjour! I see you are staring at me!
I don't mind.
My name is Escargot, and I am such a beautiful
French snail that everybody stares at me.

Right now, I am traveling to the salad at the end of this book.
It is a beautiful salad, with croutons and a light vinaigrette.

You should come!
I just need a little push
to help me start.

While we are traveling, we can talk.
Tell me, what do you think is my
most beautiful part?

My shell?

My neck?

My tentacles?

Oh là là! It is so hard to choose!
That is because all of Escargot is *magnifique!*
You can kiss me if you want.

Let's talk about our favorite animals.
Is yours the dog? The cat? The platypus?
The wildebeest? The lemur? The hippopotamus?

The snail?

Wait! Before you answer, I must tell you something sad.
So sad I might cry.
Will you stroke my shell, just until I feel better?

Okay, now I will tell you the very sad thing:
Nobody ever says their favorite animal is the snail.

Perhaps you think,
"Snails are slimy, Escargot! You are
too slimy to be my favorite animal!"
Au contraire!
The trails I make as I travel to the salad
are shimmery trails of . . .

What would you call it?
Not slime . . .
more like shimmery trails of . . .
shimmery stuff.

But enough about me.
Do you also make a shimmery trail?
What is *your* favorite kind of salad?
You look like the kind of intelligent person who
enjoys a salad with croutons and a light vinaigrette
and absolutely *no* carrots.
The kind of person who might say,
"My favorite animal is the snail!"

But perhaps you think,
"Snails are shy, Escargot! You are too shy
to be my favorite animal."
Au contraire!
I am quite fierce!

This is the face I make to scare a lion or a wild boar
or a carrot that sneaks into my salad!

Can you also make a fierce face to scare away the carrot?
Maybe we should roar at it, too!

That was a very fierce face. And a *very* loud roar.

Do you want me to come out?
Really?
Then you must say,
"Come out, Escargot!
Come out and I promise I will never put a carrot in your salad!
Come out and I will kiss you!"

Here I am!
Don't forget my kiss.
I kiss you back: *Mwah!*
Am I your favorite animal yet?

Perhaps you think,
"Snails are slow, Escargot! You are too slow to be my favorite animal."

Au contraire!
I just don't like to hurry. A French snail likes to relax before
enjoying salad with a few croutons and a light vinaigrette.
But if I *wanted* to, I could run faster than the cheetah.

You don't believe me?
I will race you to the salad at the end of the book.
Whoever gets there first will be the fantastically
fast champion of the world
and also . . .
your favorite animal.

On your mark . . .

Get set . . .

Go!

Do you see how fast I am?
I am like the wind itself.

I just need to rest for one second.
Can you blow on me to cool me off?
Okay, I am ready now for the final sprint!

I win!

Oh, you are here, too?
A tie!

We are both the champions! We are both *magnifiques*!
Let us celebrate by eating salad, with a few croutons and
a light vinaigrette.
Bon appétit!

But this is not the right salad.

This salad has a few croutons

and a light vinaigrette . . .

and CARROTS!

Escargot does *not* eat carrots.
Escargot has *never* eaten a carrot.
Escargot will now make a fierce face at the carrot.

The carrot is not running away.

Perhaps *you* would like to eat the carrot.
Go ahead, try it.
I will make you a deal: If you will try it, I will try it, too.
On the count of three we will take a very, very,
very small bite of the carrot.

One . . . two . . . three . . .

The carrot was . . . actually . . . *delicious.*
So delicious that I might have forgotten
to share.

You probably won't choose me as your favorite
animal now.
You will choose instead the baboon or the
koala or the earwig.

But that is okay. C'*est la vie.*
I will tell you a secret.
You are very beautiful
(even if you don't make a shimmery trail).
You are very fast (almost as fast as Escargot).
And you can make a very fierce face.
(Don't show me! I remember.)

You are *magnifique*!
In fact . . . *you* are *my* favorite animal.
And so, I kiss you!
Mwah!